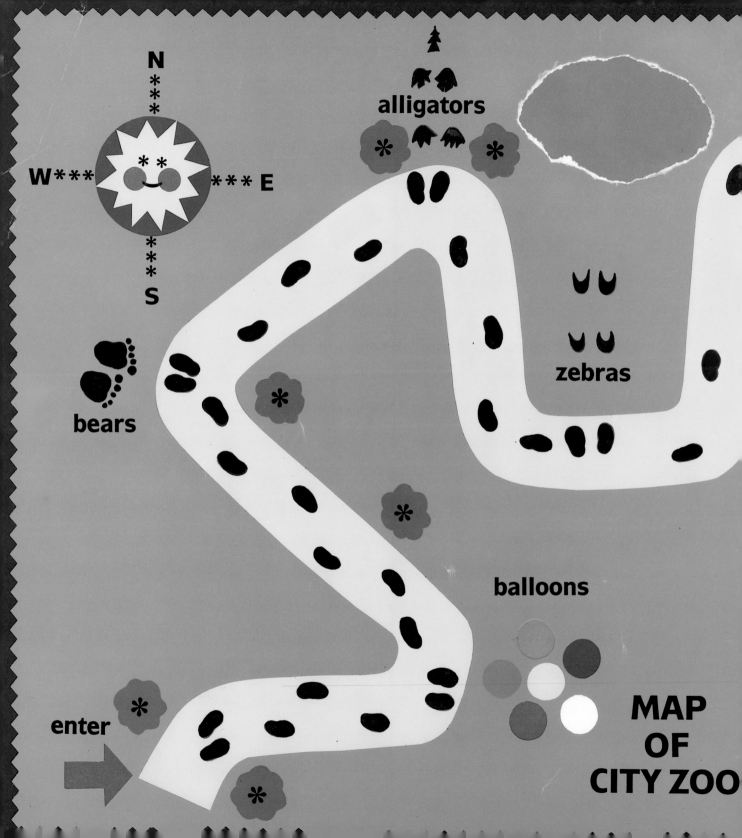

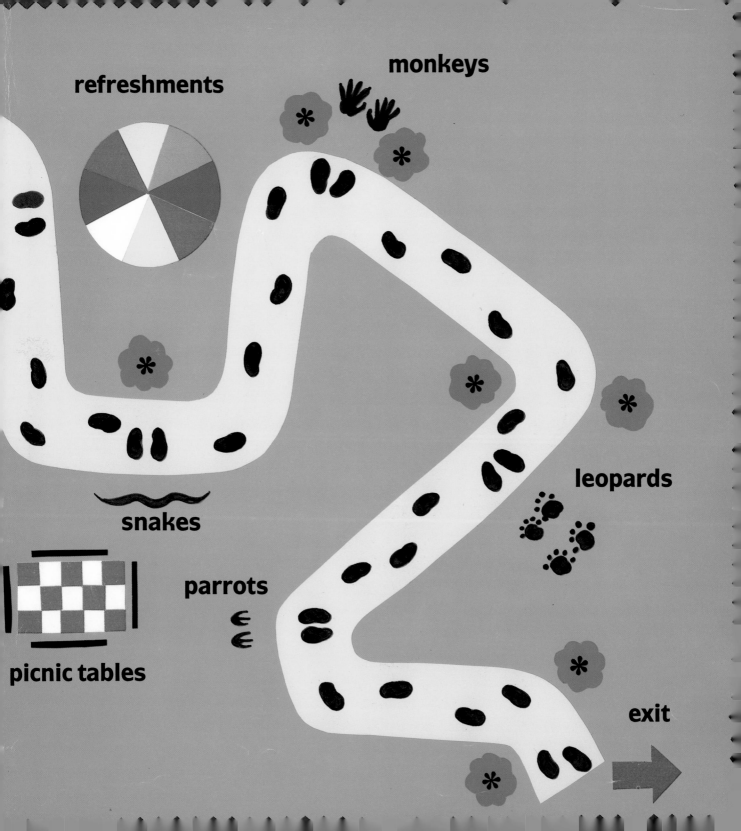

Janet Perry Marshall

My Camera

At the Zoo

Little, Brown and Company
Boston   Toronto   London

To Gordon, Elizabeth,

Andrew, Jennifer,

and Colin

Copyright © 1989 by Janet Perry Marshall

First edition

Library of Congress Cataloging-in-Publication Data
Marshall, Janet Perry.
   My camera: at the zoo / Janet Perry Marshall.
      p.   cm.
   Summary: The reader sees the zoo animals slightly askew through the camera lens and may guess what they actually are before seeing full clear views on succeeding pages.
   ISBN 0-316-54687-9 (lib. bdg.)
   [1. Zoo animals — Fiction.] I. Title.
PZ7.M356724My 1989
[E] — dc19   88 – 8376
                                                              CIP
                                                              AC

10 9 8 7 6 5 4 3 2 1

Published simultaneously in Canada
by Little, Brown & Company (Canada) Limited

Printed in Hong Kong

Last Saturday,
I took my new camera
to the zoo.

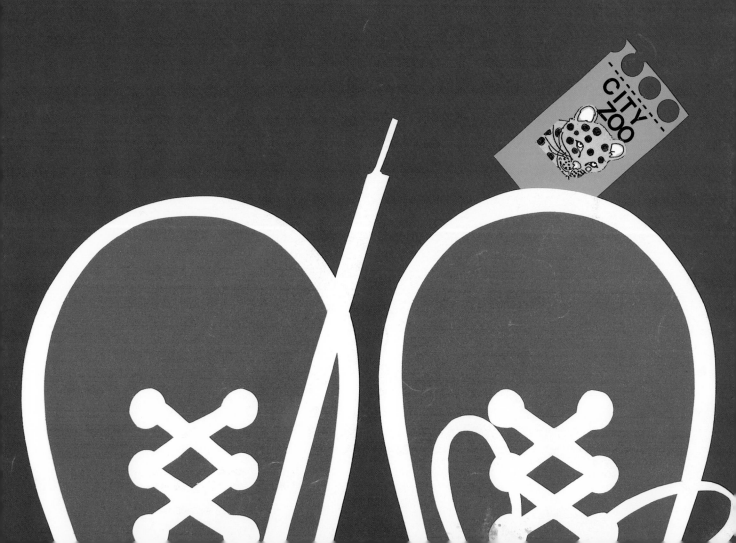

CLICK!
I took this picture first...

And then stepped back
for a second shot!

SNAP!

This fellow smiled
for me . . .

When I said "Cheese!"

POP!

I loved these licorice stripes...

Especially when someone winked back at me!

ZOOM!

I took a close-up here . . .

But kept the glass
between us!

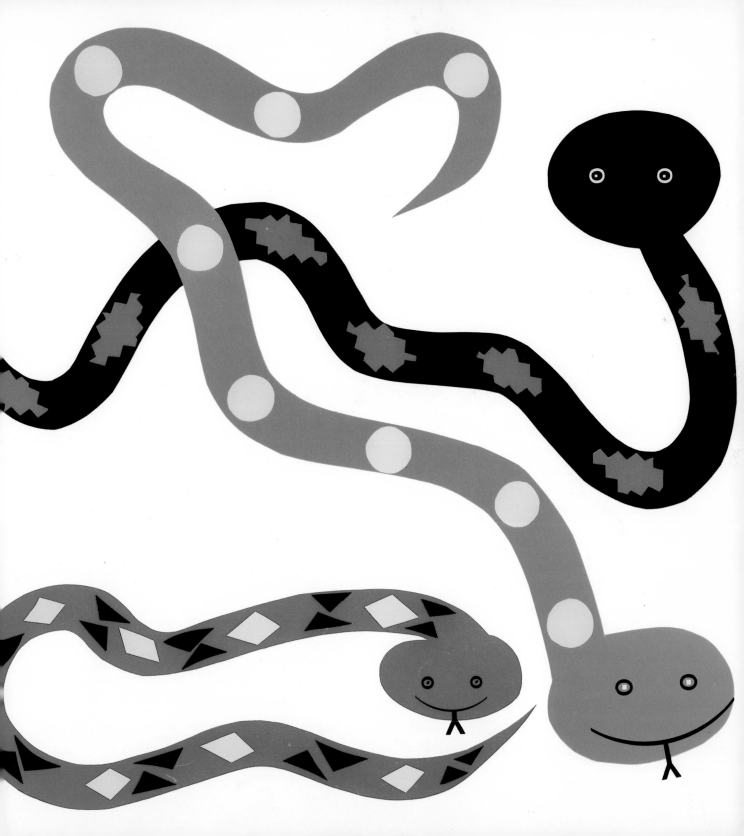

FLASH!

This little guy was upside down...

Until he turned himself around!

OOPS!

I shot this one
aiming low . . .

And then met the
proud owner of
this spotted suit!

BUZZ!

I snapped this flash of color
just before I left...

And heard this polly
squawk good-bye to me!

I'll be back again soon!

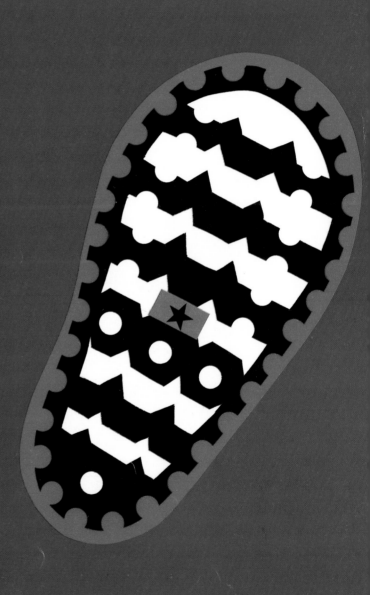
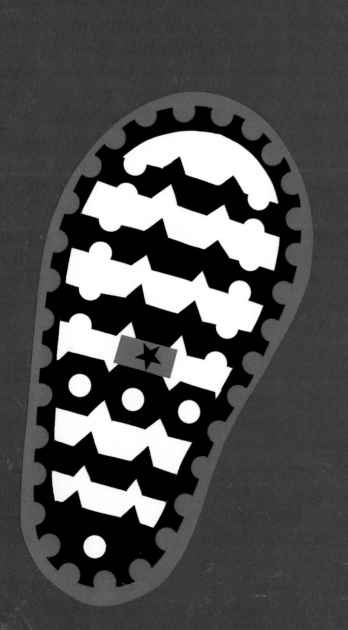